Baby Wolf

By Beth Spanjian
Illustrated by Bob Travers

A GOLDEN BOOK • NEW YORK
Western Publishing Company, Inc., Racine, Wisconsin 53404

Huddled close to their mother for warmth, five little wolf pups are sleeping soundly inside their dark den.

At dawn, the pups hear familiar whimpers.
The adult wolves have returned from the
night's hunt, bringing food back for the
family. The pups rush to greet them.

Full of energy, Baby Wolf finds a hefty stick
and drags it over to his sister.
The two of them growl playfully as they fight
over the piece of wood, tugging and pulling
with all their might. Baby Wolf yanks
the stick out of his sister's mouth.
He pulls so hard that he goes tumbling
over backwards!

As the sun gets hotter, the five pups follow
their mother to the cool shade of some trees.
There she feeds them her warm, nourishing milk.

Tired from hunting all night, the wolves
lie down for their afternoon naps.
Father Wolf lies down too, but keeps watch
over the pack as Mother Wolf sleeps.

Soon the frisky pups are up and ready to play,
but Baby Wolf pesters the wrong wolf.
Uncle Wolf growls and snaps at him!
He is in no mood for games today.

The pups explore the tall, thick grass.
Suddenly, a little mouse darts by.
Baby Wolf pounces, but he is too late.
The mouse disappears into the grass.

Baby Wolf still has much to learn about hunting.

Mother Wolf crouches down on her front paws to play with Baby Wolf. To show he is happy, Baby Wolf barks and jumps from side to side!

Back at the den, Father Wolf raises his nose
to the sky and lets out a long, loud howl.
Owoooo! The other wolves join in.
Baby Wolf tries to howl, but his squeaky voice
is too little to be heard yet.

The sun sinks slowly behind the mountain.
All of the wolves gather around Father Wolf,
wagging their tails with excitement.
To show their respect for Father Wolf,
the wolves nuzzle him and lick his snout.

Soon, the day is over. Father Wolf
starts out for the evening hunt.
The wolf pack trots behind him, one by one.
The pups stay home in their den.
They will be safe and warm until morning.
All tired out, Baby Wolf curls up next to
his sister, and falls fast asleep.

Facts About Baby Wolf

Where Do Wolves Live?

Gray wolves once made their homes in the forests and prairies throughout the continental United States, but they are now confined to only one percent of their former range. Today, fewer than fifteen hundred gray wolves exist in remote areas of northern Minnesota, Wisconsin and on Isle Royale in Michigan. Though only a few wolves live in Idaho and Montana, Alaska is still home to thousands.

What Do Wolves Eat?

Wolves are carnivores, which means they eat meat. They hunt together as a pack, so they can bring down animals much larger than themselves. Wolves will eat almost any animal, including beavers, birds, deer, moose, elk and mountain sheep. Because these animals aren't always easy to catch, wolves can go without food for several days at a time.

How Do Wolves Communicate?

Wolves are best known for their howls, but they also communicate with whimpers, whines, growls, barks and body language. The way they hold their tails, move their ears, show their teeth or raise the hair on their backs all mean different things.

How Big Are Wolves, and How Long Do They Live?

Gray wolves are the largest members of the dog family. Though baby wolves weigh only about a pound when they are born, adults can weigh anywhere from sixty to one hundred pounds or more! Wolves have lived up to sixteen years in captivity. But in the wild, seven to ten years is considered old for a wolf.

What Is a Wolf's Family Like?

A mother wolf gives birth to four to seven puppies in the spring, two months after breeding. The puppies are usually born in a den that their mother has dug into the side of a hill. After three weeks, the pups begin venturing from the den. After eight to ten weeks, they leave the den with their family and move to temporary resting spots. Not until fall, when they are old enough, can the young wolves travel with the rest of the pack. Wolves are very social and live in packs of usually four to ten family members.

What Is the Wolf's Future?

For years wolves were considered threats to livestock, big game herds and humans. Ranchers, government agents and bounty hunters killed them off one by one. Because so few exist today, wolves are an "endangered species" and receive special attention. Contrary to popular belief, the wolf poses little threat to livestock nowadays and is not harmful to people or big game herds. Wildlife managers are developing recovery plans for wolves, but their survival will depend on the attitudes of the American people.